P9-CAN-549

Board of ....ion
of Anne Arundel County

MEDIA SERVICES
Examination Copy

Elementary _____

Junior High _____

Senior High _____

Reject _____

Date Received:

SEP 5 1972

The Princess and the Unicorn

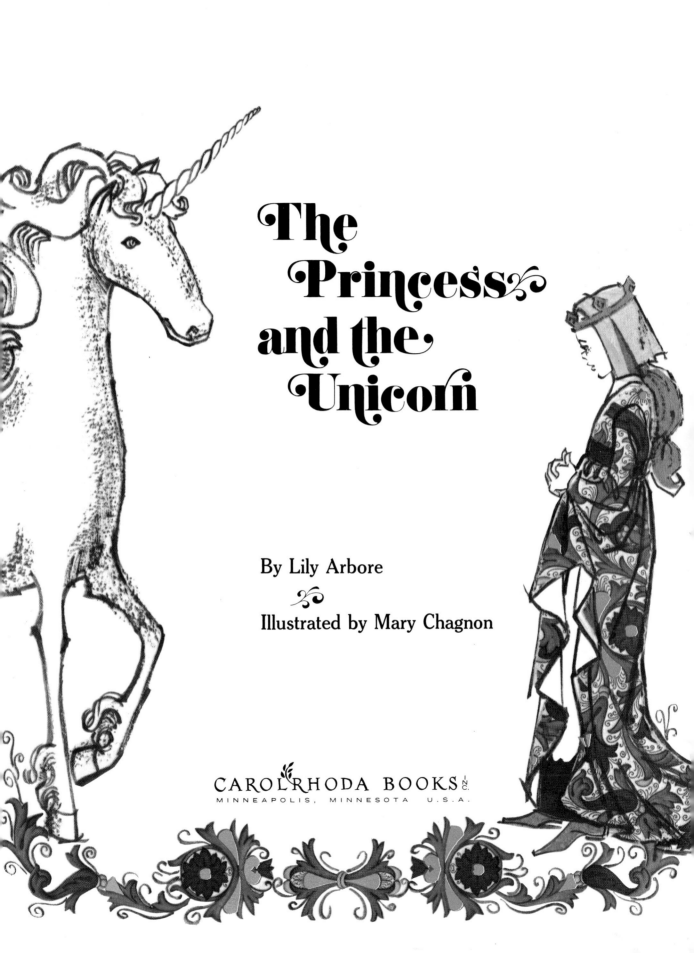

The Princess and the Unicorn

By Lily Arbore

Illustrated by Mary Chagnon

CAROLRHODA BOOKS INC.
MINNEAPOLIS, MINNESOTA U.S.A.

Copyright © 1972 by CAROLRHODA BOOKS, INC.

All rights reserved. International copyright secured. Manufactured
in the United States of America. Published simultaneously in
Canada by J. M. Dent & Sons Ltd., Don Mills, Ontario.

International Standard Book Number: 0-87614-028-2
Library of Congress Catalog Card Number: 70-171068

There lived a little Princess
In a castle on an isle,
And everyone who met her
Was enchanted by her smile.

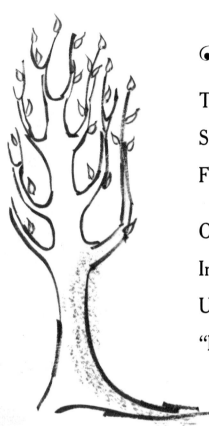

Yet when no one was looking,
There was no need to pretend.
So she'd sit and cry for hours
For she did not have a friend.

One day as she was sitting
In the garden, so forlorn,
Up stepped a stately beast who said,
"I'm Mr. Unicorn!"

They rambled among the flowers,

And they played beneath the trees,

And the Princess said "Gesundheit"

When her playmate had to sneeze.

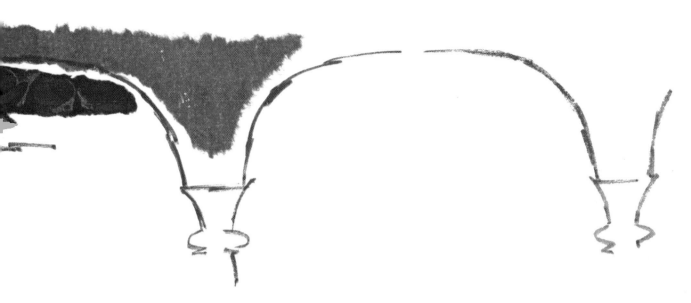

The Princess kept the Unicorn
Within the castle vault,
And she fed her friend each Sunday
A delicious chocolate malt.

One day the Princess said to him,
"Your coat is quite a sight!"
Mr. Unicorn was hurt because
She did not like him white.

She said, "Of course I love you."
But in spite of his complaint,
She decided what he needed
Was a coat of purple paint.

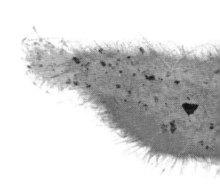

The purple-painted Unicorn
Was feeling very sad.
"If she had to paint and change me,
Why couldn't I be plaid?"

He mourned and whined and whimpered.

For hours he would cry.

At last he looked so miserable,

She feared that he might die.

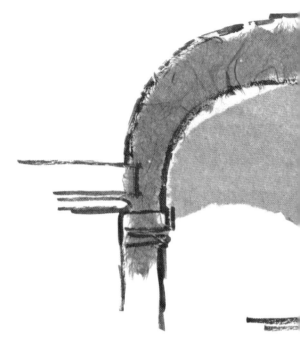

She tried a mustard plaster.

She fed him rhubarb juice.

She tried an Alka-Seltzer.

But, alas, it was no use!

"Well, I don't know what's the matter,"
Said the Princess in her dread.
She asked the King what ailed her friend,
And this is what he said:

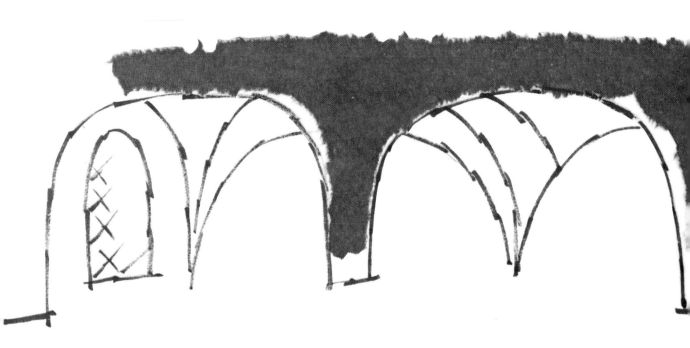

The Unicorn wants love, my dear.

You have hurt that pride of his.

The secret of REAL loving

Is to love him

As

He

Is!"

She took his words of wisdom, and
(Though it was nearly half past ten)
The Princess scrubbed the Unicorn
'Til he was white again.

Said her much befuddled friend
As she fed him caviar,
"I thought you liked me purple?"
She said, "Nope. Just as you are."

So the Princess and the Unicorn
Were once more best of friends.
They lived happily ever afterward.
That's how the story ends.

About the author

Lily Arbore is a young writer and artist who created the amusing and sensitive tale of *The Princess and the Unicorn* while still a student in high school. In addition to writing (both prose and poetry), Miss Arbore is highly interested in many kinds of handcrafts—with a special passion for weaving tapestry. Travel is her favorite leisure time activity. The author was born in St. Paul, Minnesota, and attends the Minneapolis College of Art and Design.

About the artist

Mary Chagnon is a graduate of the Maryland Institute of Art and has many years of experience as a professional fashion illustrator and pottery maker. Mrs. Chagnon worked with what has become her favorite media—paper collage—to achieve the vibrant colors she wanted for *The Princess and the Unicorn.* Her fascination with collage began several years ago when she read about the ancient Japanese craft of harié (making pictures with paper). Mary Chagnon lives with her husband, two teenage sons, and a 21-year-old parrot in Duluth, Minnesota.

CAROLRHODA BOOKS

241 FIRST AVENUE NORTH — MINNEAPOLIS, MINNESOTA 55401

Published in memory of Carolrhoda Locketz Rozell,
Who loved to bring children and books together

Please write for a complete catalogue